The Very Tired HONEY BEE

Written and Illustrated
By Tony Searle

For Smudgy.
With Love,
Papa
xx

First Published in Great Britain 2020

The Very Tired Honey Bee is an Annie in Dreamland
Story

ISBN: 9798584924089

Every night, when she snuggles down to sleep,
Annie visits a place she calls Dreamland.
A **MAGICAL** and **ADVENTUROUS** place, where anything
she wishes comes true. Annie wondered who she might meet today,
as she sighed and whispered,
"Goodnight."

It was a bright, sunny day in Dreamland.

"A perfect day to play in the garden!" Annie thought as she ran along the garden path.

Suddenly, she heard a tiny voice cry

"LOOK OUT!"

Annie screeched to a halt.
"Who said that?" she called out.

"Down here!" the tiny voice replied.
"You almost squished me!"

Right there, lying on the
ground, was a little honey
bee.

"Hello little bee. I'm sorry I almost squished you. My name is Annie," she politely introduced herself.

The little bee's wings **BUZZED** as she lifted herself off the ground.

"Pleased to meet you Annie," replied the bee. "My name is Beatrice."

Beatrice explained that her work was very tiring and she was having a little rest.

"A bee's work is never done," she said with a sigh. "There's simply not enough of us left in the hive!"

"Perhaps, I could help?" offered Annie.

"Thank you for the kind offer Annie but you are **FAR** too **BIG** to help me!"

"We can soon fix that... with a Dreamland wish!" Annie laughed.

Annie put her hands together, closed her eyes and made her wish.

"I WISH, OH I WISH, MY DREAMLAND WISH.
TO HELP OUT THIS POOR HONEY BEE.
I WILL NEED SOME STRIPES, SOME WINGS,
AND JUST ONE MORE THING...
TO SHRINK DOWN AS SMALL AS CAN BE!"

Beatrice could **NOT** believe her eyes...

Magical sparkles appeared. They **TWISTED** and **SWIRLED** around Annie like a golden ribbon.

Suddenly, **BLACK STRIPES** appeared on Annie's dress and a pair of **ANTENNAE** on her head...

She grew a delicate pair of **WINGS** on her back and then...

A cloud of magic dust, caused Annie to

SHRINK

to the size of a bee!

Annie and Beatrice flew up into the air
with a **BUZZ** of their wings.

"Firstly, we need to find some flowers,"
instructed Beatrice. "I am so tired that my super
sense of smell isn't working as it should."

"My Daddy grows flowers and vegetables at
the bottom of the garden!" Annie said
excitedly. "Follow me!"

When they reached the vegetable patch, Beatrice told
Annie what they needed to do.

"We collect **NECTAR** and **POLLEN** from the flowers," explained
Beatrice. "We carry the pollen from flower to flower to help
them grow. That's called, **POLLINATION.**"

Annie helped by blowing pollen around the flowers while
Beatrice collected the nectar.

After the work was done Beatrice said, "Now we have to take the nectar back to the hive."

Annie sang out with joy, **"WHEEEEEEEE"** as they

SWOOPED

and

LOOPED

through the air...

A huge guard stepped out from the hive's entrance.

"Oh, hi Trevor. It's only me!" Beatrice quickly answered.

"This is my friend Annie. She's been helping me collect nectar for the hive."

"Hello, Trevor," said Annie, nervously. "It's very nice to meet you. I **LOVE** your uniform!"

"Why thank you Annie," Trevor replied, blushing slightly.

"Would it be okay if I show Annie around the hive, Trevor?"
Beatrice asked.

"Anyone who helps the hive, is welcome," said Trevor. "While
you take a look around, I will announce your presence to Our
Queen."

"The inside of the hive looks **MUCH** bigger than it does from the outside." Annie thought to herself as Beatrice led her into a room filled with honeycomb.

"This is where we store the nectar we collect and turn it into honey," Beatrice explained proudly.

"It is the worker bees' job to build and take care of the hive too!" she continued.

"**WOW!**" Annie exclaimed.

"They look so **BUSY!**"

"It's very important work," said Beatrice.

"This is where we cool the nectar by flapping our wings,"
Beatrice pointed out. "It also helps to cool the hive. It can
get rather warm inside!"

Beatrice asked Annie if she would like to help seal the nectar inside the honeycomb.

"We use a sticky substance called **BEESWAX** to pack the honeycomb," explained Beatrice. "It helps to protect the nectar while it is cured into honey."

When they were finished, Beatrice said "Follow me, Annie. I'll take you to meet Our Queen."

Annie was a little nervous. She
had never met a Queen before.
She wasn't sure what to say. So,
she gave a little curtsy.

"Your Majesty,"
announced Beatrice, "May I introduce, Annie."

"Welcome Annie," said the Queen. "I hear you have been helping
our hive today."

"It's been my pleasure, Your Majesty," said Annie politely.

The Queen bee introduced Annie to her babies.

Annie cuddled a baby bee while the Queen explained that all worker bees are girls, and drones are boys.

"After I lay my eggs, I decide which eggs I will fertilise," The Queen continued. "The fertilised eggs become **WORKERS** and the unfertilised eggs become **DRONES**."

Then the Queen said, "To thank you for your help today, I would like to invite you to the 'ROYAL WAGGLE DANCE'!"

"Ooh, that would be wonderful!" Annie replied excitedly.

"I **LOVE** dancing, but I don't know how to waggle dance."

"Don't worry, Annie!" Said Beatrice, "I will teach you."

"When we find a new place to collect nectar, we waggle dance, to show the hive where to find it," Beatrice explained.
"We waggle our bodies in a figure of eight, pointing in the direction of the nectar."

Strictly Come Waggle

Annie followed Beatrice's lead.
"This is so much fun!" giggled Annie, as The Queen, and the rest of the hive looked on.

When the dance was over, the hive **CLAPPED** and **CHEERED**. "Thank you for showing us the way to your vegetable patch Annie," the Queen announced.

The Queen presented Annie with a jar of honey, as a reward for helping the hive.

"Thank you, Your Majesty, but don't **YOU** need it?" asked Annie.

"We make **THREE TIMES** more honey than we need. We are happy to share it," replied The Queen. "After all, we need you as much as you need us. So, keep planting flowers in your garden and visit us anytime!"

It was almost time for Annie to wake up.
"I've had the most **WONDERFUL** adventure!" said
Annie, giving Beatrice a tight hug.

"Thanks to you, I'm not so tired anymore!" replied
Beatrice with a big smile.
As they said their goodbyes, Annie could hear the sound
of her Mummy calling her...

"**ANNIE!** What would you like for breakfast?" Annie's mummy called from the kitchen.

"**HMM?**" thought Annie...

"Some **HONEY** would be nice!"

DID YOU KNOW?

1 Honey Bees are super fast! They can fly up to 20mph and flap their wings 200 times per second.

2 Honey Bees pollinate, Apples, Cranberries, Broccoli and Blackberries. In fact, 1 in every 3 bites of food we eat is thanks to bees.

3 Honey Bees have a brilliant sense of smell. They use this to recognise different types of flowers, when looking for food.

4 Bees pollinate 80% of the worlds plants. Without Bees, we would lose the plants they pollinate and the the animals that feed on those plants.

5 An average beehive can house 50,000 Bees. They are made up of a Queen Bee, Worker Bees (female) and Drones (male).

6 Worker Bees are responsible for collecting food and water, building the hive and regulating its temperature.

7 In some parts of the world, up to 90% of Bees have disappeared. The reason remains unknown. This is referred to as 'colony collapse disorder'.

There are many sources, for learning more facts about bees and their importance to us. Research for this story and the facts on this page, were sourced using information from: www.bbka.org.uk/pages/faqs/category/bee-facts (British Beekeepers' Association) and www.natgeokids.com/uk/discover/animals/insects/honey-bees/.

Printed in Great Britain
by Amazon